# THE
# Wish-Bringer

Written by Geraldine McCaughrean
Illustrated by Jana Diemberger

The Wish-Bringer

ISBN: 978-1-907912-06-1

Published in Great Britain by Phoenix Yard Books Ltd

This edition published 2012

Phoenix Yard Books
Phoenix Yard
65 King's Cross Road
London
WC1X 9LW

1 3 5 7 9 10 8 6 4 2

Set in Caslon and Caslon Antique

Book design by Insight Design Concepts

Printed in China

A CIP catalogue record for this book is available from the British Library

www.phoenixyardbooks.com

# THE Wish-Bringer

Written by Geraldine McCaughrean
Illustrated by Jana Diemberger

For Luca.
GM

For Lucia and the new baby.
JD

X   CHAPTER TWO   X

## IF WISHES WERE HORSES

You can't have a story without a beginning.
That would be like starting at Chapter Two.

Little Monacello knew a little of his own story; how he
had turned up one day on a doorstep, a baby packed in
a crate of straw. But that could not have been the start.

He must have begun earlier. Babies don't grow on trees
like fruit. Somewhere in Naples there must have been a
mother, a father, a birth. Somewhere, in Naples' muddled
maze of streets, lay his beginning. As soon as he was
old enough to walk, Monacello began to search for it.

There are parts of the world where people think Bad
Luck comes up from below, and Good Luck comes
down from the sky. Not in Naples. In Naples bad luck
and good came from just one place … Monacello:

Ugly little Monacello with his pasty face and pale eyes;

1

Pesky little trickster, dressed like a monk;

Lurking in the shadows, hunched and skittering;

Laughing and crying in the night;

Making mischief.

"My wife dropped a jug of milk. I bet Monacello
jogged her elbow."

"My bread wouldn't rise
this morning. I think
Monacello slept
in my stove."

"Business is bad.
Monacello must
have frightened
away all my
customers."

Monacello got
the blame for
everything.

So he made his home in the city's dank basement;
in the Undercity. To the people living overhead,
he was a dark, darting shadow, a scuffling sound
behind them, a scary glimpse. "Who's there?
Was that something? Was that someone?"

Some said the "Little Monk" was
really a ghost or a goblin.

The Frezza brothers said they had already drowned him.

The brave said they did not believe in him
at all: that there was no such boy.

Some days, Monacello thought they might be
right ... but for the cats and Napolina. His cats
must have believed in him, because they followed
him about and slept on his chest at night. And
his friend Napolina; she believed in him.

Then again, if it had not been for Napolina, he would
never have got mixed up with wishes. It was all her fault.

She kept washing his hat.

Monacello had two caps: one red, one black,
made from two pieces of cloth found in the
same crate as baby Monacello. For choice,
he wore the black cap: had much the best fun
when he wore the black cap. Whenever he put it on,
his head filled with marvellous ideas for mischief.

He was wearing a black cap the day he stole
eggs from under a chicken. He was wearing it
the day he made handprints in fresh plaster and
showed his cat friends around the fish market.

The painted walls were thorny with candle
stubs, the candlelight prickled his eyes.

Napolina would be there, stitching
another patch into her raggedy skirt.

"What have you been up to?" she
would ask in her wide-eyed way. He told her
about the eggs and the handprints.

She would say, "I think it's time I washed
your hat", snatching the black cap

4

off his head and sinking it in a tub of water.

So then he had to wear his red cap instead. Somehow, when Monacello wore his red cap, his tricks were no longer any fun.

"Find someone to be nice to," Napolina said, her smile brighter than candlelight. Then, taking one enormous breath, she blew out a dozen candles and skipped away down the dark lanes of the Undercity.

That is how he came to be sitting on a horse trough, waiting for his black cap to dry, wondering how to be nice. It was difficult: when people saw him they either ran away or threw things at him.

An old lady passed by carrying a basket of linen. She peered at the trough and tossed a little coin into the water — splip!

"What was that for?" asked Monacello, thinking
she had thrown it at him.

"Sometimes, if you throw a coin into a fountain, you get a wish."

"But this isn't a fountain. It's a horse trough," he pointed out.

"Oh, silly eyes. Silly me! Old age is a curse!" said the old lady.

"What did you wish for?" asked Monacello.

"For a horse to carry me to and from the market.
My old feet hate the walk. Now you will laugh and
call me a silly old baggage."

Monacello caught sight of his red cap reflected in the
water. "No," he said. "I won't."

When she had gone, he reached in, wetting his sleeve
right up to the shoulder, and scooped out the coin.

An ancient horse staggered by, led by a boy with a whip.
It wanted to drink from the trough, but the boy was in a
hurry.

"She's thirsty," said Monacello.

"Won't be soon, the useless bag of bones," said the boy.
"I'm taking her to the knackers' yard to be turned into glue."

"I'll buy her," said Monacello, and paid with the little coin.

He gave the horse a drink and took it to market. "Your horse," he said when he found the old lady.

She peered at the knock-kneed nag. "What a noble stallion!" she cried, clapping her hands. "My wish come true!"

Meanwhile, the hungry horse ate carrots off the Frezzas' vegetable stall. The Frezza brothers (who truly thought Monacello done for and dead) caught sight of him, gulped with fear … and then began hurling cabbages.

The hungry horse caught the cabbages and ate them, too.

As the Little Monk scuttled away, the Frezza brothers yelled after him:

"Monacello! Monacello!

Cowardy cowardy cowardy yellow;

No good hiding, ugly fellow;

We will get you, Monacello!"

"He granted me a wish!" said the old lady, still beaming.
People nearby nodded their heads. "Wishes, as
well as mischief," they said. And it was the wish
they remembered, not the cabbages or the chaos.

After that, people at their windows, on spotting
Monacello's strange, pale face and black cap,
still slammed their shutters or gave a shiver.
But sometimes, people watering flowerpots on their
balconies glimpsed a flash of red. Then softer words
spattered down on to Monacello's little scarlet cap:
"Monacello, let me win!"
"Monacello, help me find a job!"
"Monacello, bring my sailor boy safe home!"
After all, everyone has a secret wish.

8

## CHAPTER THREE

## LIVING LIKE A LORD

Poor people spend a lot of time thinking about being rich. It's strange really: the rich don't spend much time at all thinking about being poor. Avido was poor, so when he caught a glimpse of Monacello, he shouted at the top of his voice:

"Wish-Bringer Wish-Bringer,

I want to be

The Duke of Naples,

and he can be me!"

When Monacello stumbled on by without looking round, Avido threw a pebble after him.

"Just my luck; deaf as well as ugly."

But the Little Monk had heard, and because he was wearing his red cap, he could not ignore the wish.

Next morning, Avido woke up in the Duke of Naples' bed, alongside the Duke of Naples' wife who was none too pleased. Generally, she liked surprises, but she preferred them not to smell.

A lackey brought Avido breakfast in bed, on a silver tray, and opened the six chests where the Duke's clothes were kept. He drew the curtains, poured hot water into a bowl and fetched the Duchess her smelling salts. Then he bowed and went back to polishing the silver.

Through the windows Avido saw lawns and fountains, gardens and a maze, stables and a fishing lake, coaches and an excitement of servants. "Where's the money?" he asked his new wife. But the Duchess had locked herself in the sewing room.

He put on three suits and most of the Duchess's jewellery. "Well, you have to grab things while you can," he said to himself. Then he went downstairs and ate breakfast all over again.

The dining hall was hung with pictures of past dukes of Naples. Avido demanded to know why his own

11

portrait was not there. "Why should they have portraits but not me?" he asked his steward. But the steward had already gone to look for an artist.

Avido prowled through the library and rang the bell. "I am much too busy to read all these books. Find someone to read them for me."

When Avido visited the stables, the grooms brought him a tray of sugar beet to feed his favourite horse. But to their surprise, he ate it himself. "Why should a horse have sugar beet and not me?" he asked.

Meanwhile, the Duke of Naples had woken up in Avido's bed, alongside Avido's wife. (Well, Monacello had to put him somewhere.) Avido's wife was delighted.

"But I'm the Duke of Naples!" he protested.

"I don't care who you are," she said. "You're better than Avido, and you smell lovely!"

Up at the big house, councillors came to Avido with important documents to sign.

12

"Take them away!" he said. "I'm eating my lunch!"

They came to him with bills to pay: for warships and wages; for donations to the hospital; and repairs to the cathedral roof. "I'm not paying all that!" said Avido. "Do you think I'm made of money?"

They came to him with three different offers of marriage for his daughter — "I have a daughter?" — but Avido shrugged and flapped his hands: "Marry her to the one with most money."

They came to him with menus and guest lists; warrants from magistrates; petitions and begging letters; quarrels to settle; and roads to name. Minstrels wanted to sing to him. Poets wanted to read to him. His daughter wanted to cry and whimper and tell him she did not want to marry. His sons wanted money for new clothes and horses. The townspeople wanted to tell him that Monacello was up to mischief again in the city, that the Frezza Brothers were overcharging …

Avido locked himself in his library. But even there, his librarian read aloud to him in Latin, and the royal artist wanted him to sit still while he painted.

Meanwhile, the Duke of Naples went to church. "Does God want to punish me?" he asked the archbishop.

The archbishop scratched his head, bewildered. "I shouldn't think so, Sir. You are a good duke, as dukes go."

He asked the mayor of the city: "Do the people want to be rid of me? Did I let them down?"

The mayor scratched his head, baffled. "I doubt it, Your Grace. You are a fair duke, as dukes go."

His wife — or rather Avido's wife — squeezed his elbow fondly. "You must be better than the new one."

"New one?"

"I don't know who he is, but people say he's as useful as a paper hat in the rain."

So the Duke walked up to his big house on the hill and

shook hands with the guards at the gate. He hushed the maids who were sobbing, soothed the servants and grooms and officials who were fuming, and coaxed his wife out of the sewing room.

"Never fear," he said. "I am BACK."

To Avido's wife, he gave a little summerhouse in the garden and a handsome pension, because he said, being married to Avido, she had, "put up with quite enough".

Then he threw Avido (and his portrait) into the fishing lake, even though it cost him three good suits and a tiara.

As Avido splashed and spluttered and struggled, weighed down by his sodden clothes, he complained bitterly to the swans:

"Typical! That rogue Monacello grants wishes that aren't even waterproof!"

Along the wall of the orangery, a row of cats watched and wrote on their paws with the tips of their tongues, as if they might have to report back what they had seen.

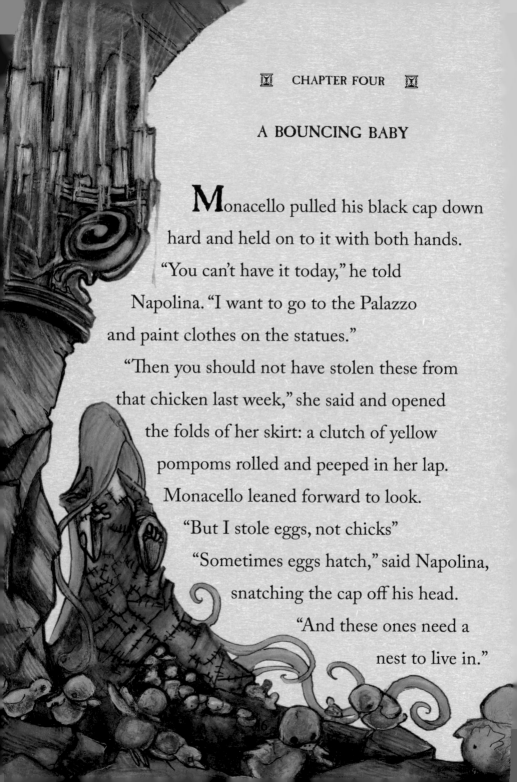

## CHAPTER FOUR

## A BOUNCING BABY

**M**onacello pulled his black cap down hard and held on to it with both hands. "You can't have it today," he told Napolina. "I want to go to the Palazzo and paint clothes on the statues."

"Then you should not have stolen these from that chicken last week," she said and opened the folds of her skirt: a clutch of yellow pompoms rolled and peeped in her lap. Monacello leaned forward to look.

"But I stole eggs, not chicks"

"Sometimes eggs hatch," said Napolina, snatching the cap off his head. "And these ones need a nest to live in."

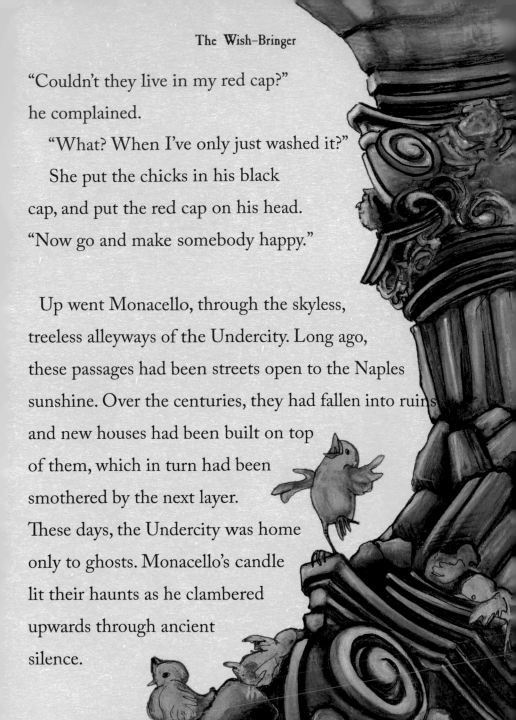

"Couldn't they live in my red cap?"
he complained.

"What? When I've only just washed it?"
She put the chicks in his black
cap, and put the red cap on his head.
"Now go and make somebody happy."

Up went Monacello, through the skyless,
treeless alleyways of the Undercity. Long ago,
these passages had been streets open to the Naples
sunshine. Over the centuries, they had fallen into ruins
and new houses had been built on top
of them, which in turn had been
smothered by the next layer.
These days, the Undercity was home
only to ghosts. Monacello's candle
lit their haunts as he clambered
upwards through ancient
silence.

His favourite secret passageway — the cats had shown no one but him — brought him out beside the Church of Santa Chiara. Inside the church, glimmering candles lit pale-faced marble statues.

Monacello thought if ever he found his mother, it would be in a place like this.

Today, there really was a woman there, in search of a baby! Kneeling in front of a lady-statue, she was praying for a child; for a baby of her very own.

Monacello did not think the stony statue would have a spare baby to give away. Besides, a baby carved from marble would be a terrible weight to carry. Why not ask for a little boy instead? A boy with two different caps, nine fluffy cats and a secret home underground! He would even throw in a hatful of chicks, if only this lady would make him her son.

The woman heard the scuff of his sandals and glanced up, face aflicker with fright. Goblin? said her eyes,

19

Demon? Then she recognised the bent Little Monk in
his lucky red cap, and quick as a wink she said:

"Wish-Bringer, Wish-Bringer, don't leave me alone!
Bring me a baby to call my own."

The statues were watching. The candles were
blinking. What choice did he have? Poor
little Monacello: if he truly was the Lucky
Boy of Naples, he had to grant her wish.

"I could bring you a hatful of chicks instead,"
he suggested, but she shook her head.

"I could bring you a kitten maybe," he offered,
but the woman pursed her lips tight.

"You could have me," he said, with a shy smile. But
she pulled a sour face. Only a baby would do.

So Monacello went out and found
the prettiest baby he could.

Just as you might go to the best cake shop in
town to buy a birthday cake, the Little Monk

went to the nicest part of town to find a baby.

He spotted one through an open window, leaned inside and picked her up. She weighed no more than an armful of spilled milk.

A door of the room opened. A nursemaid shouted: "Help! Thief! A goblin is stealing the baby!"

Her cries fetched an equerry with a fine, bright sword; a fencing master with his sharp foil; a cook with her ladle. Their shouting fetched grooms out of the stable, carrying rakes; a gardener with his pruning hook; a coachman with his whip. Guard dogs broke free of their tethers and came bounding. Monacello set off at a run.

Despite the barking, the shouting, the shrieking, the bouncing about, the little baby slept on in Monacello's arms.

21

Over bridge and stile went the Little Monk, though farmhands, huntsmen and a troop of soldiers all joined in the chase. On he scampered ... until the tiny, hungry streets and alleyways of old Naples swallowed him down like a cherry stone.

All evening the sound of heavy boots thumped about the city. All night torches flared in the streets. But no one thought to look in the Church of Santa Chiara. Only the statues saw Monacello deliver the wish.

"I brought you a baby," he said, when at last he could catch his breath.

The woman stared at him. "What's this?"

"It's your wish. You wished for a baby."

"Yes. A baby of my own! This one is second-hand!"

"It's a very nice baby."

"Are you mad? I can't just arrive home with a baby! People would say I stole it!"

"Tell them you wished for it."

The baby began to cry; a noise so loud that the

22

stained glass shook in the windows. Hurriedly, she gave the bundle back, like a loaf taken too hot from the oven. "And it's a girl," she shouted. "I wanted a boy!"

"Did you put the baby back?" asked Napolina. "Did you take her home?"

"Yes, and she was very heavy," Monacello said and threw his red hat on the floor. He had been looking forward to telling Napolina about his wasted journey, the ungrateful lady, the long trek back lugging a baby half as big as himself. As usual, Napolina seemed to know already.

"Foolish little monk. Babies are not like horses."

"They're just as heavy," complained Monacello. "I'm not doing any more wishes."

"I heard a girl wish on you today."

Monacello shut tight his crooked little mouth.

"And a young man, too," said Napolina. "He was sighing like the wind."

Monacello tipped the chicks out of his black cap and put it on his head. "I am Mischief-Maker

Monacello," he said and glared, daring her to stop him.

Napolina only shrugged her skinny shoulders and danced away into the dark. "All right, then. Tomorrow, why don't you steal a ladder?"

The chicks swirled about the floor like dandelions on legs. The cats watched them hungrily. Can cats wish too? wondered Monacello.

"Now, Hairdrop! Stop that, Fleahouse!" he said sternly, but the cats only licked their furry lips. So, folding his two caps one inside the other, and putting the chicks safely back in their nest, he balanced them high out of reach.

Then he lay down on his sagging, sacking bed, and his faithful friends jumped aboard, sheltering Monacello from the draughts and the loneliness and the Big, Bad Dark.

## 🖂 CHAPTER FIVE 🖂

### ROBERTO AND ROSETTA

Monacello could not see the fun in stealing a ladder ... until he saw Fippo Frezza in his garden, picking peaches. The Frezza Family hated him. As dogs hate cats, as cats hate rats, as rats hate traps, so the Frezzas hated Monacello. The very sight of him made their fists clench. Their hate was as long and spiky as the alphabet; they had chased him from A to B and out to sea. They had pelted

him with eggs and peas, but they had never said why.

Usually, the Little Monk was too quick for
them. Usually, they missed. But now and then a
tomato left pips in his hair. Now and then some
of the hate stuck , and hate did not wash out.

So while Fippo was clambering about the huge tree in
the garden of Frezza Mansion, Monacello tiptoed away
with the ladder and left him squawking like a parrot.


Now Monacello could go and paint moustaches
on the tallest statues in Naples! He set off down the
narrow street, knocking and hooking, hoiking and
hitting, splitting and tilting, turning and tipping,
and toppling everything ahead and behind.

Monacello, causing chaos as usual.

But that morning, unknowingly, he had put on both
his caps — the red and the black — because one was
still tucked inside the other. So, when he heard the
strains of a love song coming from an upstairswindow,
the magic word "wish" brought him to a halt.

"I wish I was hers.

I wish she was mine.

With sweet Rosetta

Life would be fine!"

It was Roberto the ballad singer.

"No, no," thought Monacello. "Mischief tonight, wishes tomorrow."

But further up the hill, he passed under a balcony and heard a woman's whispered wish, and because he was wearing both his caps, he could not help but hear it out.

"Oh Monacello, little fellow,

If I saw you I would tell, oh

How I love my dear Roberto

Let us marry, Monacello!"

It was the easiest wish in the world to grant. Rosetta loved Roberto, but her greedy father wanted her to marry a rich husband, and kept her shut up tight, like his money. Roberto wanted to marry Rosetta but dared not ask, because all he could offer were music and love.

All they needed was a
ladder to set them free!
Monacello was annoyed.
Now the statues would have to
wait. He went back to Roberto's
house, climbed up his stolen
ladder and shook the shutters.
Roberto and Monacello carried the
ladder through the streets to Rosetta's
house and set it against the balcony.
Up went Roberto, to knock at
the shutters. Down came bride
and groom with nothing but a
silvered hairbrush and a warm
coat for luggage. Waiting below was a
carriage to carry them out of the city.
Two wishes granted at a stroke.
Monacello's pale eyes swirled with pleasure
and he threw both his caps in the air.

It was Fippo Frezza who caught them.

Stepping out of the shadows, all five Frezza brothers barred the street. Fippo wore a velvet cloak, a silly grin and a tangle of peach twigs in his hair.

"Rosetta, you lucky girl! I am ready and willing to marry you"

Halfway down the ladder, Rosetta looked round with a start. "Oh, but Fippo, my heart already belongs to Roberto. We love each other! I cannot marry you!"

Fippo gave a snort. "Your father says that you can, and I agree with him. Shall we say tomorrow, at noon?"

"You can say what you like," exclaimed the plucky Rosetta, "but I say never! You cannot make me marry you!"

Fippo's face set as cold and hard as a frozen pond. "But you will do … unless you want to see your little songmonger die on my sword point here and now." With a harsh rasp, five silver swords were drawn from their sheaths.

Rosetta screamed.

Roberto clung to the ladder.

The ladder shook with their trembling.

But Monacello's pale eyes flashed dark a temper as
huge and terrible as magic

The clouds turned inside out. A chimney fell.

Flowerpots tumbled from the balconies and
smashed at the feet of the Frezzas. The carriage horses
reared in their traces. The sweethearts leapt on to
the coach's roof as the horses set off at a gallop.

The Freeza brothers tried to snatch the reins -
to stop the carriage from speeding away, but
their feet were suddenly aswirl with cats, and
the ladder toppled, blocking their path.

Only the Little Monk remained, small and
frail, face as white as a saucer of milk, trapped
and helpless, smiling a twisted smile.

"I thought I killed you once, goblin," spat Fippo.

"Maybe once was not enough," said Monacello,
pulling himself to his feet.

Pointing a finger at the Little Monk, Fippo laughed a snarling laugh.

"I remember the night another man climbed from a balcony just like this, don't you brothers? Shall I tell him about the pest who came to woe our sister?"

Why, all of a sudden, did Monacello tremble at those words? No one loved stories more than he, so why did he want to stuff his fingers in his ears?

Why now, beneath that balcony, did his bent little body stop stock still, like a little question mark faced with an answer?

## CHAPTER SIX

## A FATHER FOUND AND LOST

"We were waiting then, too, eh boys?"

Fippo's brother's shuffled their feet,
wiped their noses with their hands.

"Name of Marco. Chipped stone for a living."

"A sculptor."

"A sculker, more like."

"Came skulking into our garden night after night."

"Trying to steal our silly sister's heart."

"Like a burglar."

"Couldn't stay away."

"Till we caught him one night, eh brothers?"

"We did, Fippo."

"And put a stop to him." Fippo's lip curled.

His brother's nodded, remembering the night they
have flung their sister's admirer out of Naples with
kicks and curses: "We decide who joins this family!"

"Come back here and we'll kill you!"

Fippo licked the blade of his sword from guard to tip, as though he was licking an icicle. "And do you think we ran that pest out of Naples, only to let you plague us instead? You? His goblin son!"

Five blades flashed, and so did the lightning.

But Monacello's pale eyes flashed brighter. "You banished my father?"

Throughout the city, every shutter in every house banged.

The clouds clashed like cymbals.

Church bells clanged.

Dogs yowled and howled.

Starlings shoaled in a jumbled sky. And every cat's tail tied itself in a knot.

Remember, said those knots. Remember the Frezzas banished Monacello's father!

Fippo put away his sword. "No need to dirty our blades, brothers. This is the Wish-Bringer." And pointing a finger at the Monacello, he chanted:

"I wish I may,

I wish I might

See you in your tomb tonight!"

And what could he do, the little Wish-Bringer, but grant Fippo's wish?

## CHAPTER SEVEN

## DEAD AND GONE?

The funeral was like a parade, with music and drums, masks and flags. People came to their windows, crowds ventured out of doors.

"Whose funeral?"

When they heard it was Monacello, some were glad. "No more mischief!"

But some were sad. "No more wishes."

Through the streets the procession wound, with whistles and drinking songs instead of hymns; torches and dancing instead of tears. Behind it trailed a thread of cats, each with a knot in its tail.

It came at last to a graveyard, where Fippo took
an iron bar and prised opened a tomb. Inside it they
laid Monacello, the Good-Luck-Bad-Luck boy.

No words of goodbye.

No prayers for his soul.

Only a wreath of cats yowling on top of a sealed tomb.

And a feeling in the air as heavy as a sick horse

… a stolen baby

… a lonely heart.

"Monacello is dead!" The Frezzas chant it round
the streets of Naples. Their wish has been granted,
they say, by the
Wish-Bringer himself.
"Monacello is dead!"

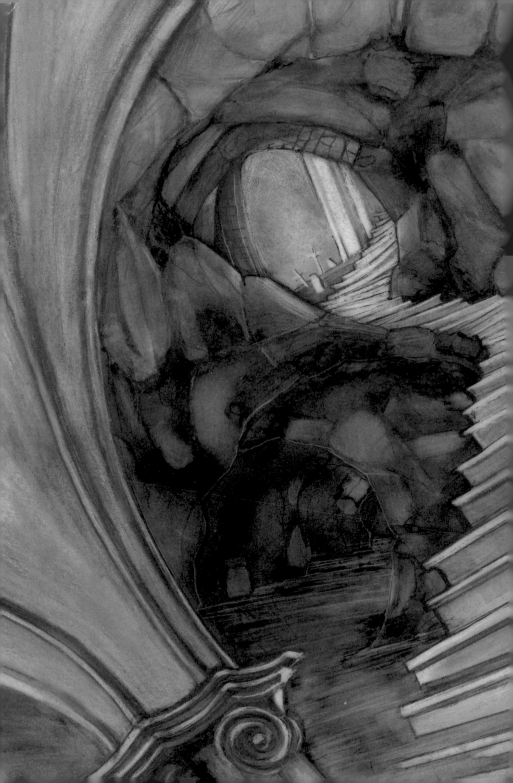

But wait a minute! Which churchyard was this?

Just where was that dismal tomb?

In the darkness, fur brushed Monacello's trembling hand; fur and a knotted tail.

"Fleahouse? Where did you spring from?"

Where else but that hole in the paved, stone floor – those worn steps – that ancient passage sloping down and towards and forgotten, buried city...

Inside Santa Chiara Church, nine marble Madonnas smiled to hear the soft scuffle of sandaled feet skittering down stairs.

In the Undercity, in the room with a sun on the wall, Monacello sits like a king among his courtiers: Wormy and Fleahouse, Hairdrop and the Admiral.

His head is bare now that both his caps have fallen into the hands of his enemies. It is no longer possible to tell if he has mischief and good luck in him.

Remember, say the knots. Remember to make the Frezzas pay.


Ancient, anxious ghosts peep in at the door and glide sadly away.

Perhaps it is they who fetch Napolina, because suddenly there she is, as cheerful as honeysuckle, her apron full of chicks.

"Make a wish, Monacello."

"Me?"

"Of course you! Surely the Wish-Bringer is allowed one wish for himself? And everyone has a wish. Don't you?"

His milky eyes curdle with the bitterest thoughts,
but Napolina lays a finger to his lips.

"Only one, mind. So make it a good one."

Her face is thin and tired. Her lips are as pale
as marble. She has no more home or family
than he does. She is as poor as the poorest
beggar in Naples. Yet she has never
asked him for a wish of her own.

Monacello breathes in and says, "I wish …

What will you wish for, little Monacello; strange
boy, pale-eyed and as bent as a question mark?

Will it be for mischief or revenge?

"I wish…" he said, "I wish…
I wish that you would ask me for a wish."

Napolina laughs with delight. "Oh that's
easy! I wish I knew the rest of your story!"

"But I don't know that myself!"

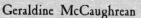

"Then I wish you'd find out," says Napolina.
And she carries the little ones away —
upwards and up — to show them
their first light of day.

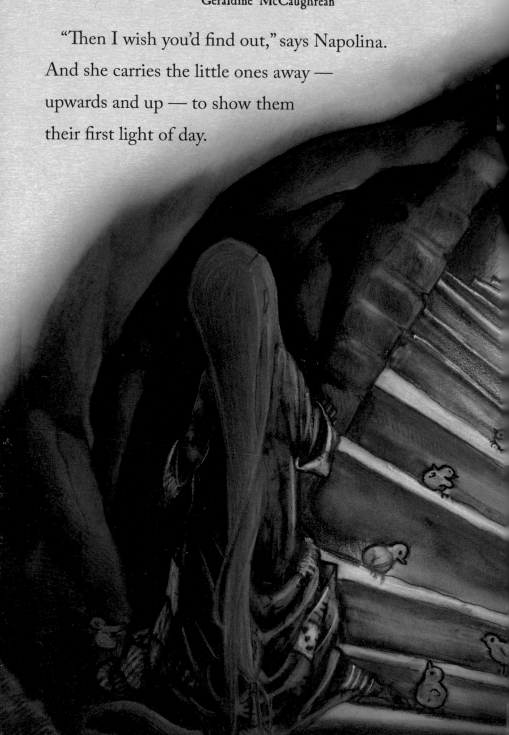

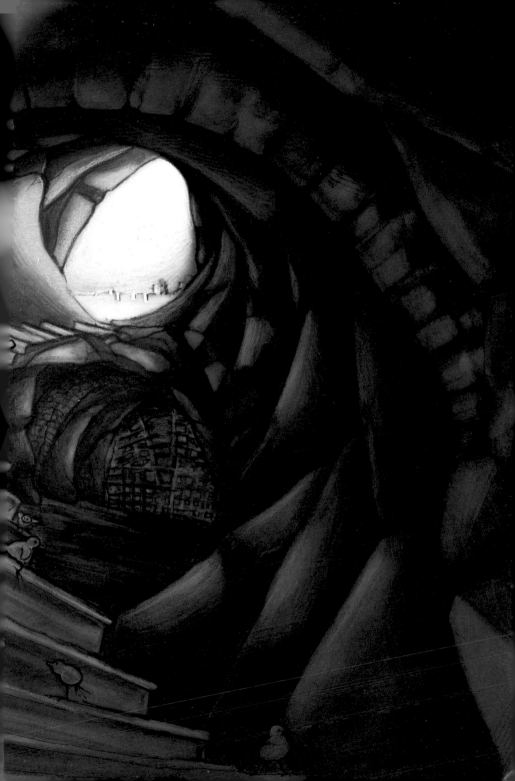

## MONACELLO: THE LITTLE MONK

It all began with a knock at the door and no one there...

# Monacello

### THE LITTLE MONK

Written by Geraldine McCaughrean
Illustrated by Jana Diemberger

## ANYTHING BUT PERFECT

Amid the strangers and dangers of Naples, lies
the secret Monacello longs to find. Perhaps it will
explain why the Frezza brothers hate him so much.
Perhaps it will fetch him up again into the sunshine.
But is he brave enough for the truth?
Some secrets are so terrible it may be better not to know.
Brave? Of course he is brave! He's King of the Undercity!
Afraid? Of course he's afraid. He's only little. In
the meantime, Naples goes on peeping through
its shutters, heart thumping, watching for
Monacello, the Good-Luck-Bad-Luck boy.